The Boy with Flowers in His Hair

For Jenna

First published 2022 by Walker Books Ltd
87 Vauxhall Walk, London SE11 5HJ

2 4 6 8 10 9 7 5 3 1

Text and illustrations © 2022 Jarvis

This book has been typeset in Didot

Printed in China

British Library Cataloguing in Publication Data: a catalogue record
for this book is available from the British Library

ISBN 978-1-4063-9251-7

www.walker.co.uk

WALKER BOOKS
AND SUBSIDIARIES

LONDON • BOSTON • SYDNEY • AUCKLAND

The Boy
with
Flowers
in His
Hair

JARVIS

His name is David.
He's the boy with flowers in his hair
and he's my best friend.

Everybody likes David. Even Mrs Jones,
and flowers make
her sneeze.

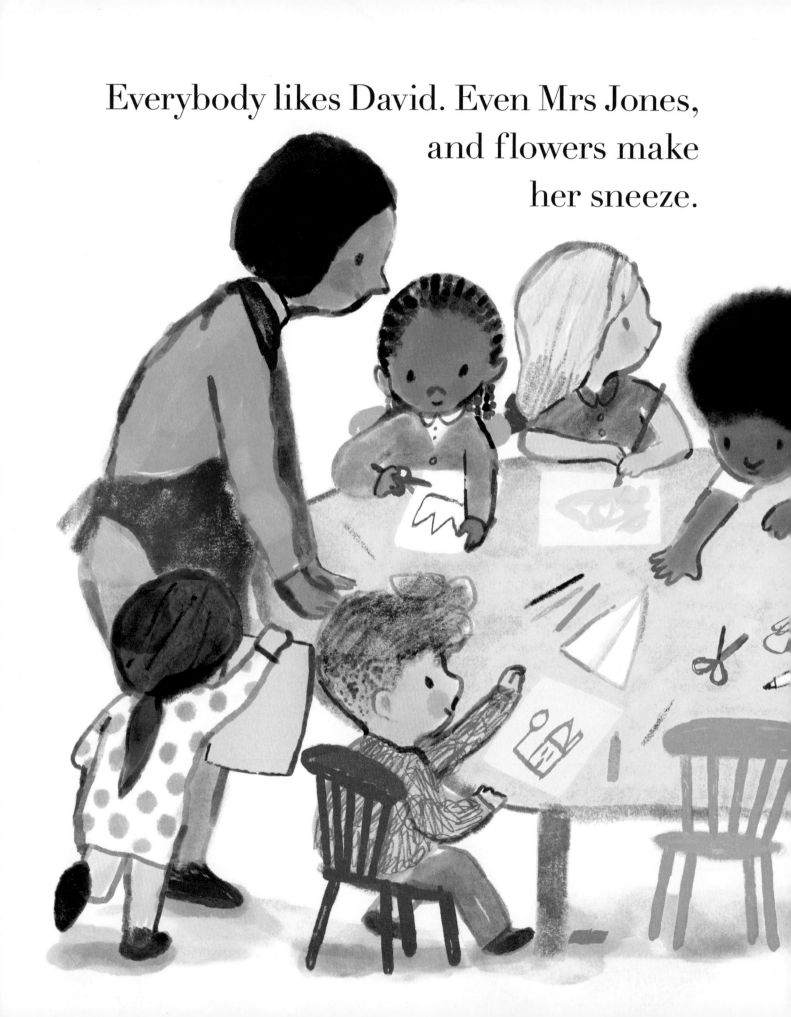

He's sweet and gentle, just like his petals.

We have the best time together ...

finding the
good puddles,

making up songs,

and running away
from the bees.

Once, he had a family of birds
living in his hair for a whole month.
It was really funny.

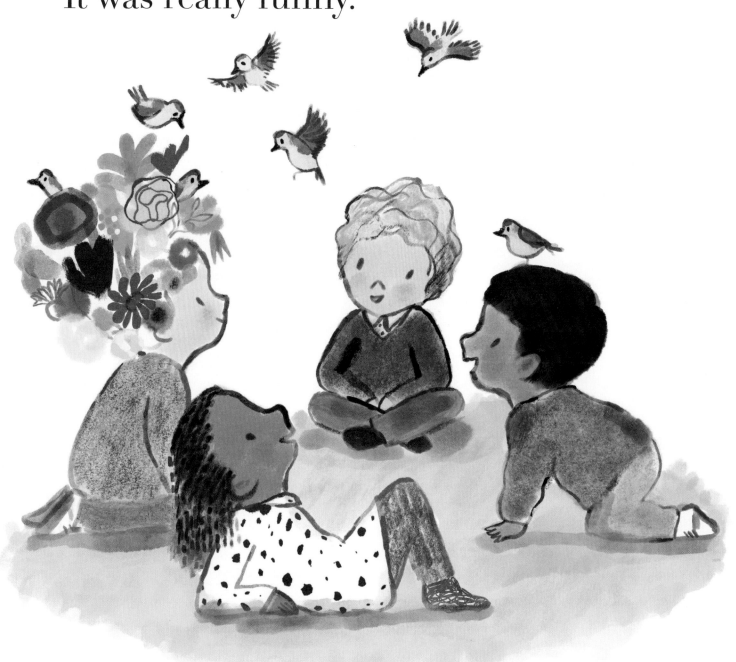

But one day, something happened.

I was watering David's hair
and one of his petals came off
in my hand.

That afternoon, he didn't want to play.

The next day, he started wearing a hat.
David never wore hats.

He was quiet.
David was *never* quiet.

Mrs Jones asked us to take off our coats and hats and scarves.

When David took off his,
petals fluttered down like butterflies.
David was twiggy, spiky and brittle.

Everyone stayed away,
in case they got hurt by his branches.

I got a few scratches,
but it wasn't David's fault.

Then I had an idea.

I asked Mrs Jones for a paintbrush,

and some scissors,

and I found a way ...

to give David
his colour back.

I made new flowers for David all the time.
Everybody wanted to help.

David seemed back to how he was before.

Almost.

Then, one day,
I noticed a different flower in David's hair.

It wasn't one of mine.
It wasn't one of anyone's.
It was David's.

It was a real flower,
a new flower,
prettier than ever.

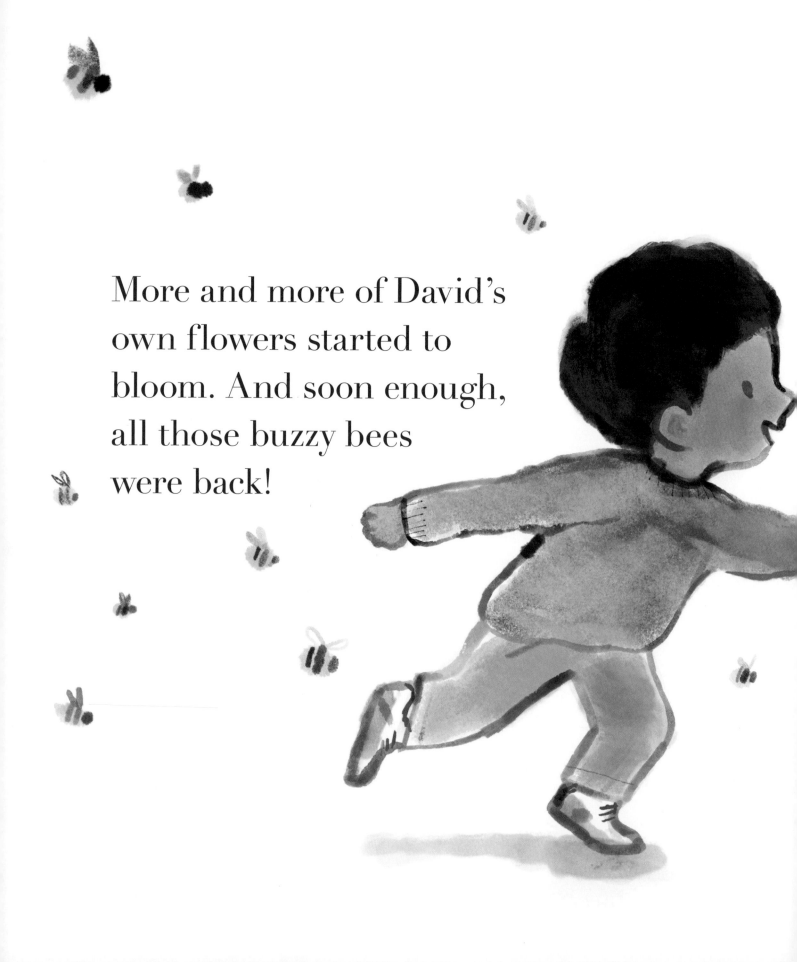

More and more of David's own flowers started to bloom. And soon enough, all those buzzy bees were back!

So, right now,
David has lots and lots of flowers
in his hair.

But I'm making sure I still have
lots of paper ones just in case
he ever needs them.

Because he's my best friend,
and I am his.